MW00902425

JANE YOLEN

Hoptoad

ILLUSTRATED BY
KAREN LEE SCHMIDT

Silver Whistle

HARCOURT, INC.

SAN DIEGO   NEW YORK   LONDON

www.HarcourtBooks.com

Silver Whistle is a trademark of Harcourt, Inc.,
registered in the United States of America and/or other jurisdictions.

Library of Congress Cataloging-in-Publication Data
Yolen, Jane.
Hoptoad/Jane Yolen; illustrated by Karen Lee Schmidt.
p. cm.
"Silver Whistle."
Summary: A toad barely escapes being squashed beneath the wheels of a car.
[1. Toads—Fiction. 2. Stories in rhyme.] I. Schmidt, Karen, ill. II. Title.
PZ8.3.Y76Ho 2002
[E]—dc21   2001001229
ISBN 0-15-216352-2

First edition
A C E G H F D B
Printed in Singapore

The illustrations in this book were done in watercolor and gouache on Winsor & Newton cold-press paper.
The display type was set in Vag Rounded.
The text type was set in Futura Medium.
Color separations by Bright Arts Ltd., Hong Kong
Printed and bound by Tien Wah Press, Singapore
This book was printed on totally chlorine-free Enso Stora Matte paper.
Production supervision by Sandra Grebenar and Pascha Gerlinger
Designed by Linda Lockowitz

To my new grandson
—J. Y.

For my father, Norman, and my brother, Paul
—K. S.

Hoptoad.

Hop—toad!
Hop, hop
across that road.

Wide road.
Side road.

Truck coming.

Heavy load.

Toad hop.
Toad hop!

Oh no—

don't stop.

Hop toad,
fast, faster.

Here comes

toad-al disaster.

Toad?

Whew toad,

now you've
slowed.

Hop toad,

off that road.